Legends

OF CHRISTMAS

Georgianna Summers

C.S.S. Publishing Co., Inc.

Lima, Ohio

THE LEGENDS OF CHRISTMAS

9044 / ISBN 1-55673-256-2   PRINTED IN U.S.A.

| *Production Notes*

This drama can make use
of all the children in a Sunday school. Junior and senior high youth
can take the main parts; older elementary children can dramatize the Babushka legend; primary children can dramatize the na-
tivity pageant; pre-school children can play the animals around the
manger. The size of the play cast is flexible, using as few as ten
or as many as fifteen. For instance, some of the parts can be dou-
ble cast. Robbie could play Nicholas; the crying woman in the
Boniface legend could be taken by the girl who plays Mama, and
so forth. All conversation parts should be memorized, but the
legend reports can be read.

The play can be presented on a stage or in a church sanctu-
ary with a minimum of scenery. The stage area should be divided
into three sections — a classroom area on one side, a locker area
on the opposite side, and a playing area in the middle. If space does
not permit, the locker and playing areas can be the same. Lockers can simply be two screens with lockers drawn on newsprint
taped on them. There should be a chalkboard on a wall or an easel
in the classroom area, positioned so that the audience can see
what is written on it.

The Legends of Christmas

Scene i

[Members of a junior high Social Studies class are seated on one side of stage area. Miss Hardgrader, the teacher, stands in front of them.]

Hardgrader: Now, class, before you leave today I just want to remind you that your reports on Christmas legends are due tomorrow. *[Everyone groans.]* I will call on some of you to read yours aloud; so all of you come prepared. I've also invited the other grades in our wing to come visit our class tomorrow when you give your reports, and I thought it would be fun to sing a few Christmas carols together and make it a kind of party.

Marcia: *[Raising her hand]* Should we come in costume, Miss Hardgrader? *[Class members mutter disgustedly.]*

Hardgrader: Well, you can if you like, Marcia, but it's not necessary. Now, if there are no other questions, you may all go. *[Class rushes out. Derek and Robbie stay behind to talk to Miss Hardgrader. Danny, Marcia, Becky, and Katie stop at locker area and pretend to open their lockers.]*

Danny: Boy, what a dumb question that was, Marcia. This is Christmas, not Halloween.

Marcia: So? What's wrong with wearing a costume to dramatize your legend?

Danny: Well, I'm sure not wearing any dumb old costume.

Katie: You don't need to. Just wear those patched-up pants you've got on, and you'll look like a tramp.

Danny: Hey, man, these are my favorite pants. They've got class.

Marcia: Ugh! *[Works at her locker during next few lines.]*

Becky: *[To Katie]* Did you see that cute boy on the bus yesterday?

Katie: Did I ever! Did you get his name?

Becky: I think it's Duke.

Katie: I wonder if he's going with anybody?

Danny: *[In disgust]* If he's smart, he isn't.

Becky: Is that so? Well, you're not smart, and I don't see you going with anybody.

Katie: Of course not. Who'd be caught dead going with him? Come on, Becky. Let's try to be first on the bus so we can sit next to Duke.

Katie: *[As they go out]* Oooh, he's so cute.

Danny: *[Mimicking them behind their backs]* Oooh, he's so cute. *[Derek and Robbie come out of classroom area to locker area. Miss Hardgrader exits.]*

Robbie: *[Full of gloom]* Some Christmas party tomorrow's going to be.

Derek: Do you have your legend, Robbie?

Robbie: I don't even know what a legend is. *[Turns to locker.]*

Marcia: *[Turning from her locker]* Robbie, according to Webster, a legend is a story from the past that is often taken as historical fact but is not verifiably true.

Danny: Now that makes about as much sense as anything else you ever say, Marcia.

Marcia: *[Giving him a withering look]* I am writing on the legend of the Christmas rose. What are you doing, Derek?

Derek: I thought maybe something to do with King Arthur and the Holy Grail.

Robbie: Are you sure that's about Christmas?

Derek: Well, maybe not strictly speaking, but after all, Christmas is about Jesus, and the Holy Grail was the cup he used at the Last Supper; so maybe with a little explanation and elaboration —

Robbie: *[Holding his head]* Good heavens!

Marcia: Have you got a legend yet, Robbie?

Robbie: Uh — well, I — uh — all I've got is a headache.

Marcia: And I don't suppose *you've* come up with anything, Danny?

Danny: That's all *you* know. There's one right there in our Social Studies book about how in old England the maids told the man-servant to bring in some holly to deck the halls, and if he didn't they punished him by stealing his trousers and nailing them to the gate.

Marcia: That isn't a legend. That's just a custom.

Danny: It's the same thing.

Marcia: No it isn't. Honestly, Danny, you are so dumb. Miss Hardgrader won't accept that, and you won't get a grade on your report. Well, that's your problem. *[She flounces off.]*

Danny: *[Shouting after her] That* isn't my problem. My problem is being in the same class with you. *[To Robbie and Derek]* Boy, I pity the poor guy she marries.

Robbie: What makes you think anybody will marry *her*?

Derek: Who knows? Maybe someone will marry her for her money.

Danny: I doubt it. There's not that much money in the world. Now because of dumb old Marcia I've gotta go home and come up with something else for my report. Come on, guys.

Robbie: *[As they go out together]* I think I'll go home and take an aspirin.

Derek: I'm stopping by the library to look up King Arthur and the Holy Grail. *[Lights out momentarily]*

Scene ii *(The Next Day)*

[Lights up. A boy comes in and draws a funny picture on the chalkboard. Labels it "Miss Hardgrader." Another boy joins him and draws a heart with "Marcia loves Danny" on it. Other students enter and go into classroom, talking quietly. "Artists" go into classroom when they finish. Becky and Katie enter into locker area, talking to each other.]

Becky: Oh, I was never so embarrassed in my whole life.

Katie: *You* were embarrassed. What do you think *I* was?

Becky: Well, how did I know she was his girlfriend? I just thought she was some girl who had sat down next to him.

Katie: You didn't have to ask her to get up so I could sit there.

Becky: I had to think of some excuse. Besides that, you were the one who wanted to sit next to him.

Katie: Me! You were the one who thought he was so cute.

Becky: Who cares? I like Tom better, anyway. *[Robbie enters.]*

Robbie: Are you girls still talking about boys? Honestly, don't you ever think of anything else?

Katie: What else is there to think of?

Robbie: Legends, that's what. They're due this period, and I'm doomed. I suppose you girls have yours all ready.

Becky: Yeah, I've got something about mistletoe.

9

Robbie: That figures. *[Marcia enters wearing a long skirt and a dust cap. Robbie pretends to open his locker.]*

Katie: Who are you supposed to be?

Marcia: You'll see. *[Danny enters.]* Well, did you finally come up with a real legend? *[Katie and Becky go into classroom.]*

Danny: *[Yawning]* Yes, I did, Smarty. Stayed up half the night looking, but I found something just as good as yours. Mine's about St. Nicholas. What's yours about, Robbie?

Robbie: Well, uh, mine's about — it's — oh, have I got a headache!

Marcia: We'd better get to class before Miss Hardgrader marks us tardy. *[They start into classroom. Derek comes running in wearing a crown and carrying a sword.]*

Becky: Good heavens. Who's he supposed to be?

Danny: King Arthur. Who else? *[Sits down on front row in classroom area. Miss Hardgrader enters.]*

Hardgrader: *[Noticing chalkboard]* Well, I see we have some new art work on the chalkboard. A perfect likeness. Anybody know who the artist is? *[Everyone points to Danny who denies it loudly.]*

Marcia: *[Noticing the heart]* Who did that? *[She gets up and erases it. Students snicker.]*

Hardgrader: Time to settle down, class. I see some of you have come in costume today. From the looks of things we should have some interesting legends about Christmas. *[Turns to audience]* I'd like to welcome our guests, and in keeping with the spirit of the season, I think it might be nice to intersperse our legend reports with the singing of carols. The words are printed on your programs. Why don't we start out with "Deck the Halls." *[During the singing of this, Danny yawns, stretches, and goes to sleep.]*

Hardgrader: *[After carol is sung]* Since we've been singing about decorating with holly, I wonder if anyone came up with a legend about holly? It seems to me, Danny, that you were interested in this yesterday. *[Louder]* Danny? Have you got something about holly?

Danny: *[Sleeping]* Go get it yourself. *[Everyone snickers.]*

Robbie: I think he's asleep, Miss Hardgrader.

Katie: Sounds like he's having a nightmare.

Hardgrader: I think you may be right, Katie. Let's not disturb his dream. If no one has a legend about holly let's turn in your Social Studies book to page 63 and see what it says there about holly. Would you read it to us, ____ ? *[During the reading of this, Marcia, Katie, and Becky move to the center of the stage area as part of Danny's dream.]*

Student: *[Standing and reading]* One of the legends about Christmas is that when Christ was born in Bethlehem the bees sang praises to him, and that is why bees hum to this day. Because of this legend it was long a custom in England to put a sprig of holly in each beehive at Christmas. The English also like to decorate their houses with holly, and in the big manor houses in merry old England it was the job of the servants to see that this was done.

Marcia: Hurry up, girls. We have to get this hall cleaned and decorated before the party tonight.

Becky: We can't decorate until that lazy Danny brings the holly in.

Marcia: Did you tell him to?

Katie: I told him, but all he said was "get it yourself."

Marcia: That does it! He will have to be punished.

Becky: Oh, goody! Do we get to steal his pants?

Katie: I'll go sneak them out of his room. *[She goes out.]*

Becky: And this means he won't get to kiss any of us under the mistletoe this year, either.

Marcia: Who cares? Who wants to kiss him anyway? *[Katie comes back in carrying a pair of patched jeans like the ones Danny is wearing.]*

Katie: Here are his pants. Let's go nail them to the gate. *[They go back to classroom, hiding the pants under a chair as Danny starts to wake up.]*

Danny: *[Shouting in his sleep]* Give me back my pants! Give me back my pants! *[He wakes up.]* Where am I? *[Stands up and points to Katie.]* You stole my pants. *[Sits down.]*

Katie: I did not!

Hardgrader: Danny, you fell asleep. You must have had a bad dream.

Danny: Did I ever! It was a nightmare. Marcia and Katie and Becky were all in it.

Hardgrader: Well, now that you're awake perhaps you'd like to share your Christmas legend with us. What is it about?

Danny: It's about St. Nicholas.

Hardgrader: Good. Why don't we all sing "Jolly Old St. Nicholas" while you're getting yourself awake. *[During the singing, a student who plays Nicholas goes offstage and slips on a robe or surplice and a miter. Student who plays Papa also leaves and can put on a sleeveless jerkin over his shirt and trousers.]*

Danny: *[Standing and reading]* St. Nicholas was a bishop who lived during the fourth century in Asia Minor. He was a very good man, and one of his chief traits was his generosity. One of the most popular stories about his good deeds was about a nobleman who had three daughters. *[Katie, Becky, Marcia, and another girl who plays Mama go offstage to get a rocking chair and sewing basket, bring them back on and take their places in the center — Mama on the rocker, pretending to sew, daughters grouped around her.]* These three daughters all wanted to get married [naturally] and in those days a girl couldn't get married unless her father paid the poor dude who was going to marry her a lot of money. This was called a dowry. They probably did this because all the girls were ugly and bossy and no one would marry them unless they were paid to.

Becky: Sisters, did you notice that handsome gentleman at the marketplace yesterday?

Katie: Did I ever! Did you get his name?

13

Becky: No, but I think he's a duke, and he was talking to Papa.

Katie: Maybe he was asking Papa for your hand. You are almost old enough to be married now as soon as Papa can find a suitable mate for you.

Marcia: Oh, I hope Papa finds someone handsome and rich and young for each of us. Do you think he will, Mama?

Mama: Now, girls, I'm sure your father will do his very best for each of you. Here he comes now. *[Papa enters, looking very dejected. Mama jumps up.]* Husband, what's the matter? Something has happened.

Papa: I'm afraid so. My business deal with the duke has fallen through. All our money is lost.

Mama: Oh no! Is there nothing left?

Papa: Only enough for us to live on if we live very frugally. All the servants must go.

Marcia: Does this mean there is no money for our dowries?

Papa: I'm afraid that's right. *[The daughters all start to wail loudly.]*

Becky: Oh no! Now we'll never get married.

Katie: We'll all be old maids. Oh, I wish I were dead.

Mama: Now girls, we must just make the best of our situation. Come, let's go to bed and perhaps things will look better in the morning. *[Everyone exits.]*

Danny: *[Continuing to read]* Word of the nobleman's bad luck reached the ear of Bishop Nicholas, and when the oldest daughter reached marriageable age, he went to their home one night and threw a bag of gold through a window. *[Nicholas sneaks in and throws bag of gold. When he leaves, Becky enters.]*

Becky: *[Picks up bag and opens it.]* Mama, Papa, Sisters. *[They come running in.]* Look — gold for my dowry! Where did it come from?

Papa: I don't know, but God be praised.

Mama: Now, daughter, you will be able to marry well.

Danny: *[Continuing]* And so she did. *[Becky takes bag and goes back into classroom as Danny continues to read.]* When the next daughter reached the age to marry, Nicholas repeated this kind deed, and she also married well. *[Katie goes back to classroom.]* Then finally it came time for the third daughter to marry. She was the bossiest and the ugliest, so she needed a lot of money.

Marcia: Oh, Mama, I am old enough to be married now. I wonder if our unknown friend will leave a bag of gold for me.

Mama: I don't know, daughter. I wonder who this friend is.

Papa: I am going to find out. Now that our third daughter has reached the age to marry I am going to keep a close watch each night to see if I can catch our friend in the act. *[Marcia and Mama exit into the classroom. Papa hides in a corner of stage area.]*

Danny: *[Continuing]* And so the nobleman kept watch each night, and soon Nicholas came by. *[Nicholas comes in to throw bag. Papa jumps out and grabs him.]*

Papa: Aha! So it is you who has been so kind to us. I am so grateful, dear bishop, that I want everyone in the city to know what you have done.

Nicholas: Please, friend, do not tell anyone. I would rather give my gifts secretly. *[They exit together to remove their costumes.]*

Danny: *[Continuing]* But the nobleman was so grateful that he could not keep the secret, and so stories of the bishop's generosity spread, and whenever unexpected gifts arrived he was given the credit. One version of this story was that one of the bags of gold fell into a stocking that was hung up to dry by the fireplace; so that's where the custom of hanging up stockings at Christmas comes from.

Hardgrader: That was excellent, Danny. *[As he takes his seat he turns and sticks his tongue out at Marcia.]* I wonder if anyone else has a different legend about St. Nicholas, or Santa Claus, as we call him. *[Student raises hand.]*

Student: I have a legend from Russia about Babushka, who is kind of like Santa Claus.

Hardgrader: Good, _____ . Why don't we stop and sing a carol before your report. How about "Silent Night"? *[During the singing, older elementary children who are dramatizing the Babushka legend take their places backstage. The students who played Papa and Nicholas return to the classroom minus their costumes.]*

Student: *[Standing and reading]* My legend is about Babushka, who was an old grandmother in Russia. *[Babushka enters and sits in rocker.]* It was in the winter, and she was sitting in her rocking chair by the fire. Suddenly she heard a knock on the door. She got up and went to the door and found some shepherds there. *[She does so.]*

Shepherds: Grandmother, Grandmother, you must come quickly. There is a baby born in the stable at Bethlehem. You must come and take care of him and his mother. *[The shepherds' lines can be said individually or in unison.]*

Student: *[Continuing]* But it was warm by the fire and Babushka did not want to leave her warm house and bed.

Babushka: I will come tomorrow. *[She goes back to rocker.]*

Student: Then the shepherds knocked again. Babushka went back to the door. *[She does.]*

Shepherds: Please, Grandmother, if you cannot come yourself, will you fill up a basket of food? We will take it to the stable. The baby and his mother may need it.

Babushka: *[Shaking her head]* Tomorrow will be soon enough.

Student: Then the shepherds went away and Babushka went to sleep by the fire. *[She returns to rocker.]* When morning came she packed a basket of fruit and cakes and meat. *[She gets up from chair, takes the sewing basket and pretends to pack it.]* She also put in a shawl for Mary and a silver spoon for Jesus and some toys for him to play with. Then she went out to the stable. *[She leaves.]* But the stable was empty; so ever since then, Russian children believe that Babushka wanders all over the world from town to town on Christmas Eve looking for the stable with the Christ child and Mary. *[Several children enter.]*

17

Child: Do you think Babushka is out looking for the Christ child tonight?

Child: I hope so.

Child: I hope she will leave something for me.

Child: Me, too. But she won't if we don't go to sleep. *[Children lie down and sleep. Babushka enters, reaches into her basket and pretends to leave something for each child as student continues to read legend.]*

Student: Whenever she comes across a good child who is fast asleep, she reaches into her basket and leaves three gifts — one that is useful, one to play with, and one to eat. *[Children and Babushka leave as student sits. Someone from class removes rocker.]*

Hardgrader: That was very interesting, _____ . Now I wonder, Derek, if we shouldn't hear from you. Judging by your costume, I would gather that it has to do with King Arthur.

Derek: Well, actually it has to do with Boniface and the legend of the first Christmas tree, but since Boniface was from England and King Arthur was from England, I thought they were related enough for me to come dressed as King Arthur. There was really only a couple of hundred years between the two.

Hardgarder: As close as that, huh?

Marcia: *[In disgust]* Really, Derek, they have nothing to do with each other.

Hardgrader: That will be enough, Marcia. Let's hear your legend, Derek.

Derek: *[Standing and reading]* My legend takes place in the deep, dark forests of Germany in the eighth century, when terrible, ferocious beasts lurked behind every tree as in the days of King Arthur when Pellinore came to Camelot in search of the questing beast, and he stayed on and warned Arthur —

Marcia: *[Loudly]* Honestly! *[Class members all say "Sh-sh-sh"]*

Derek: Anyway, the people in that part of the world were druids, and the chief god they worshiped was Woden. Then, after the days of King Arthur, people in England who were Christians sent missionaries to Germany, and one of them was named Boniface. *[Boniface enters in monk's robe and faces the class. Derek sits down.]*

Boniface: And that, my friends, is the story of Jesus.

Katie: That's a beautiful story. We have never heard about that kind of god.

Becky: Doesn't your god want a human sacrifice?

Boniface: What do you mean?

Marcia: We druids believe that the god of light and fire lives in a huge oak tree in the middle of the forest. We call this tree the Woden Oak.

Student: Every year one of our finest youth is sacrificed at the Woden Oak. I myself have given up one of my sons to be sacrificed.

Boniface: What a terrible thing! That must have brought you deep sorrow.

Student: It did. But we have no choice. We must do it or the god will be angry.

Boniface: December must be a very sad month for all of you; whereas we Christians find it the happiest month of the year because it is the month we celebrate the birth of Jesus. In England we celebrate his birthday by decorating our houses with holly and evergreen branches and singing songs about his birth.

Student: We have a celebration in December, too, for our gods.

Student: Yes, we honor our chief god Woden by tying apples to tree branches to honor our sun god, Balder, because we want him to return. *[Sound of someone sobbing.]*

Boniface: What is that? It sounds like someone crying. *[Woman comes in.]*

Student: It is the wife of our chief.

Boniface: What is wrong, good woman?

Woman:*[Crying]* The tribesmen have come for our oldest son. They have taken him now to offer as a sacrifice at the Woden Oak.

Derek: *[Continuing his narration]* So Boniface started through the forest to stop the pagan sacrifice. *[Boniface goes to center area, followed by class members as Derek continues.]* The people were very frightened because they were afraid he would make the god whom they believed lived in the tree angry and that something terrible would happen to all of them. Finally, they came to the huge oak tree. *[Two boys come out, one with his hands bound; the other holding him and about to stab him with a knife.]*

20

Boniface: Stop! There is no god who lives in this tree. Instead there is a God of love who sent us Jesus who taught us how to love each other. This tree has no power over you. *[Boy is released and runs to his mother; rest of the class shrink back in fear and horror.]*

Derek: So the legend says Boniface cut the tree down, and there behind it was a fir tree.

Boniface: See this evergreen tree. Call it the tree of the Christ child. Take it into your homes and decorate it with the fruits and cakes and lighted candles that you offer to your pagan gods. Make it instead a symbol of life and joy in honor of the God who loves you and wants you to live. *[Boniface leaves; class return to their seats.]*

Derek: So when the druids became Christians they continued their winter celebrations, but they changed them to honor Christ. And the evergreen tree came to symbolize new life.

Hardgrader: That was very good, Derek, even if it didn't have anything to do with King Arthur. What better song to sing now than "O Christmas Tree"? *[Audience sings.]* Now, Robbie, I wonder if you have a legend you'd like to share with us?

Robbie: Oh, boy, does my head hurt!

Hardgrader: What's that, Robbie?

Robbie: Nothing, Miss Hardgrader.

Hardgrader: Well, do you have a legend to report on?

Robbie: *[Standing]* Uh — well — uh — I don't exactly have a legend, but I was thinking that there are a lot of things about celebrating Christmas that have to do with the first Christmas — like that legend about Babushka.

Hardgrader: *[Encouraging]* Yes, Robbie? What did you have in mind?

Robbie: *[Gaining confidence]* Well, I was thinking that we put stars on top of our Christmas trees because the wise men followed a star. And we give gifts maybe because the wise men brought gifts to the manger. Why we wouldn't even be celebrating Christmas or have any legends about it at all if it hadn't been for the first Christmas.

Hardgrader: You're absolutely right, Robbie. I think perhaps this might be a good time to sing "The First Noel." If we sing all the verses that are printed, it will tell the whole story of the first Christmas. And maybe our younger classes could act it out for us as we sing.

[Verses 1 and 2: Shepherds enter; pretend to sleep. Angels enter; shepherds wake up. All leave during second chorus. While they are leaving, someone brings manger out and Mary and Joseph take their places behind it.]
[Verse 4, "This star drew nigh, etc.": Mary and Joseph stand behind manger during this verse.]
[Verses 3 and 5: Wise men enter and offer gifts; leave during last chorus. Mary and Joseph remain.]

Hardgrader: Now, _____ , let's hear from you. What is your legend about?

Student: *[Standing]* My legend is about the animals who were in the stable that first Christmas. There was a cow, and the donkey that Mary rode, and some sheep that the shepherds brought. *[Pre-school children in animal hoods enter and stand around manger.]* The legend is that because Jesus was born in a stable, stables are sacred places on Christmas Eve. And, at the stroke of midnight on Christmas Eve, all the animals in stables everywhere kneel down and worship the manger. Some versions of this legend say that the animals can speak then, but they only do this if no human beings are around.

Hardgrader: Very good, _____ . Why don't we sing "Away In a Manger." *[Pre-school children leave during last verse.]*
And now, _____ , I'd like for you to give the legend you were telling me about yesterday.

Student: *[Standing]* My legend is called "The Legend of the Christ child's Birthday Party." It says that on Christmas Eve two special angels are sent to earth to gather up sleeping children who are especially good and take them to heaven just for that evening to celebrate the Christ child's birthday. *[Teachers get all the children back into the stage area.]* When they get there they have a party. They play games with rainbows for hoops. They play catch with the stars. And the halls of heaven ring with their laughter and the sound of their music.

Hardgrader: *[Bringing out birthday cake]* What should we sing, children?

Children: *[Shouting]* "Happy Birthday." *[They and class members sing "Happy Birthday" to Jesus.]*

Hardgrader: And that, of course, is what Christmas is all about. Before the bell rings, why don't we *all* join the party and sing the first verse of "Joy to the World." *[Audience joins the cast in singing.]*

www.ingramcontent.com/pod-product-compliance
Lightning Source LLC
Chambersburg PA
CBHW071232130626
46555CB00004B/1950